Published by Hachette Partworks Ltd.
ISBN: 978-1-908648-96-9
Date of Printing: November 2013
Printed in Malaysia by Tien Wah Press

From the movie

DISNEY
FROZEN

Disney

Hachette

The kingdom of Arendelle was a happy place, next to a deep fjord. At night, the northern lights lit up the skies in beautiful patterns.

But the king and queen had a secret worry.

Their eldest daughter, Elsa, had magical powers. She could freeze things and create snow, even in summer!

Their youngest daughter, Anna, adored her elder sister. The two loved to play together in the snowy playgrounds that Elsa created.

One night, Elsa's magic accidentally hurt Anna.

The king and queen rushed the girls to the realm of the trolls for magical help. The trolls said Anna would recover. They also advised that Elsa's powers would get stronger, so she should learn to control them.

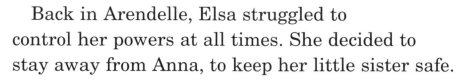

Back in Arendelle, Elsa struggled to control her powers at all times. She decided to stay away from Anna, to keep her little sister safe.

The trolls had changed Anna's memories, so she didn't remember Elsa's magic. She grew up thinking that Elsa wanted nothing to do with her.

By the time Elsa was crowned queen, the sisters hardly knew each other.

Having grown up mostly by herself, Anna was lonely. She was thrilled to meet handsome Prince Hans on the day of Elsa's coronation.

Anna and Hans liked each other right away.
At the coronation party, they danced and talked
all night.

Anna told Elsa that Hans wanted to marry
her as soon as possible.

"How can you marry someone you just met?"
said Elsa angrily.

Anna argued back. "I can't live like this anymore!"
Then Elsa got upset and an icy blast shot from
her hand – in front of everyone!
Worried that her secret was out, and
afraid she would hurt someone, Elsa fled.
Everything froze behind her as she ran.

Once Elsa climbed into the mountains, she
calmed down. All alone, she could let her powers
out for the first time! She created whirls of snow,
ice and even an ice palace. She could be herself,
and it felt wonderful!

Meanwhile, Anna realised that Elsa had been acting distant all these years because she had to hide her magic. Anna decided to go after Elsa – now her secret was out, they could be together!

Anna headed up the mountain. Then her horse threw her into the snow. Luckily, she found shelter.

Inside, Anna met a young man covered in frost. He was grumpy because he was an ice harvester and the midsummer snowstorm was ruining his business.

He knew where the storm was coming from. That meant he could take her to Elsa!

Anna hired the young man, Kristoff, to take her up the North Mountain to find Elsa. His reindeer, Sven, came along too.

As they neared the top of the mountain, the trio saw a beautiful wintry landscape. Elsa had covered everything with colourful, sparkling ice.

Elsa had also created
a snowman… who was
alive! His name was Olaf.

Olaf was excited to hear that Anna
planned to bring back summer,
because he loved the idea of warm
weather. He volunteered to take
them to Elsa.

The group continued
on and finally, they
found the fantastic ice
palace that Elsa had
created with her magic.

Anna was impressed by Elsa's powers. She asked Elsa to come home. But Elsa thought the people of Arendelle wouldn't accept her – and she was still afraid of hurting them. The girls argued.

Although Elsa didn't intend to hurt Anna, she hit her sister in the chest with a blast of ice.

Then she created another snowman, named
Marshmallow, who was much bigger than Olaf. The
snowman made sure that Anna, Kristoff and Olaf
left the mountain quickly!

Kristoff noticed that Anna's hair was turning white. He took her to the trolls, to ask them if they could help her.

The trolls explained that Elsa's blast had hit Anna in the heart. Soon, she would freeze completely! But they added, "Only an act of true love will thaw a frozen heart."

Olaf and Kristoff hurried Anna back to Arendelle so she could get a true love's kiss from Hans.

Back in Arendelle,
Hans helped everyone
during the storm. Then
Anna's horse returned
without her!

Hans took a group out to find Anna…
but found Elsa first. Elsa had to defend
herself from the men. Finally, she was
taken back to Arendelle – and put in
the dungeon! The men were convinced
she was dangerous, but they didn't
want anyone hurting Elsa.

Kristoff brought Anna to Arendelle, but Hans refused to kiss her. He didn't love her after all! He wanted to rule Arendelle and had to get the sisters out of the way first.

Anna was devastated. But Olaf realised that Kristoff loved Anna – so his kiss could still save her. Anna made her way toward Kristoff. Then she saw her sister in danger...

She threw herself in front of Elsa, just in time to block a blow from Hans' sword.

At that moment, Anna transformed into solid ice. The sword shattered against her icy body.

Stunned, Elsa threw her arms around Anna and cried. Suddenly, Anna began to melt!

Elsa's act of true love meant that the spell was broken. Then Elsa managed to bring back summer.

The sisters hugged and promised to love each other. The people of Arendelle welcomed Elsa home.

Kristoff stayed in Arendelle, and so did Olaf – with the help of a little winter cloud to keep him cool. Best of all, the sisters were together again and happy at last!